THIS BOOK BELONGS TO:

_____

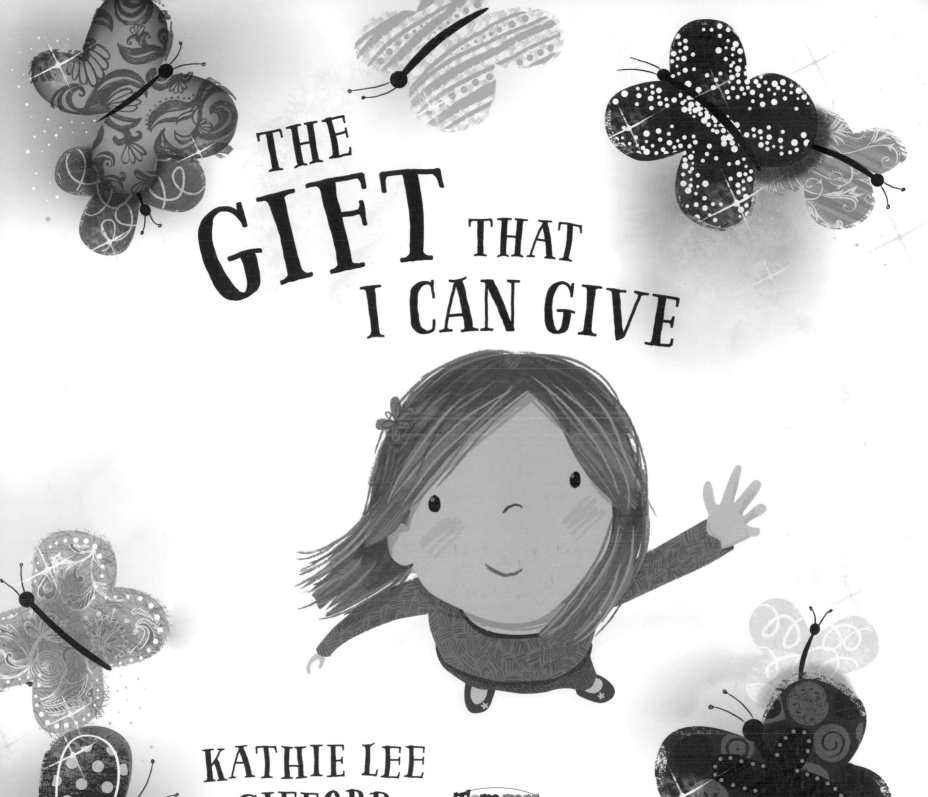

THE
GIFT THAT
I CAN GIVE

KATHIE LEE GIFFORD

ILLUSTRATED BY
JULIA SEAL

Tommy
NELSON

An Imprint of Thomas Nelson
thomasnelson.com

Published in Nashville, Tennessee, by Tommy Nelson. Tommy Nelson is an imprint of Thomas Nelson. Thomas Nelson is a registered trademark of HarperCollins Christian Publishing, Inc.

Illustrated by Julia Seal

Tommy Nelson titles may be purchased in bulk for educational, business, fund-raising, or sales promotional use. For information, please e-mail SpecialMarkets@ ThomasNelson.com.

ISBN 978-1-4002-0924-8

Library of Congress Cataloging-in-Publication Data is on file.

Printed in China

18 19 20 21 22   DSC   10 9 8 7 6 5 4 3 2 1

Mfr: DSC / Shenzhen, China / October 2018 / PO # 9500363

This book is lovingly dedicated to
Aaron "Shecky" and Zachary,
the two newest members of our family.
I can't wait to see the gifts God grows in you.

I'm one of a kind—
I'm my very own *ME*!
Exactly the person
God made me to be!

When I was small,
Right from the start,
God poured out a gift
Deep **down**
in my heart.

What is this gift
To use as I grow?

When will I see it?
How will I know?

God, will You show me
This gift I can give
As I grow and love
And I learn how to live?

Could my gift be
A wonderful thing,

Like having the talent
To dance or to sing?

Or could my gift be
Giving my all
And helping my team
By **passing** the ball?

There are so many things
That I'm really good at . . .
But what if **my gift**
Is much different from that?

Maybe my gift
Is just to be kind
By taking care of
Stray animals I find.

Maybe my gift
Is to **cheer** on a friend

So he can run that race to the end!

Or maybe my gift
Is to lend a hand
While keeping the beat
With the marching band!

Get Well Soon
x

Or to **visit a sick child**
In a hospital bed
Or to raise some money
So hungry kids are fed.

Or to give my family
An **extra-big** squeeze . . .
Is it possible that my gift
Is all of these?

All God asks me
As I grow, love, and live
Is that I show others
The gift I can give.

Then He'll help me find ways
To give it away
As He lives in my heart,
Every moment, every day.

His love is the **gift** that I can give!